Wide Awake

Volume I

Ukiyoto Publishing

All global publishing rights are held by

Ukiyoto Publishing

Published in 2022

Content Copyright © Ukiyoto

ISBN 9789364940023

All rights reserved.
No part of this publication may be reproduced, transmitted, or stored in a retrieval system, in any form by any means, electronic, mechanical, photocopying, recording or otherwise, without the prior permission of the publisher.

The moral rights of the author have been asserted.

This is a work of fiction. Names, characters, businesses, places, events, locales, and incidents are either the products of the author's imagination or used in a fictitious manner. Any resemblance to actual persons, living or dead, or actual events is purely coincidental.

This book is sold subject to the condition that it shall not by way of trade or otherwise, be lent, resold, hired out or otherwise circulated, without the publisher's prior consent, in any form of binding or cover other than that in which it is published.

"And one day she discovered that she was fierce, and strong, and full of fire, and that not even she could hold herself back because her passion burned brighter than her fears."

- Mark Anthony, The Beautiful Truth

CONTENTS

Poem By Tanmayi Arora	1
Poem By Rojalin Mahapatro	5
Short Stories By Shruti Sinha	10
Short Story By Vidya Premkumar	18
Short Story By Sristi Sengupta	31
Short Story By Priyanka Joshi - More	44
Short Story By Dipayan Chakrabarti	58
Short Story By Juju's Pearls	72
Poem By Ekta Singh Chandel	87
Short Stories And Poem By Deep Wilson	90
About the Authors	*116*

Poem By Tanmayi Arora

Wide Awake

An empowered woman stands awake
Along with chaos the conditions break
She calls for the changes to take place
The explications and solutions she always encase

Gone is the era when she covered her face
Now are the days she creates her own place
She embarks and leads the world
She flipped her strategies and the dice turned

She is the healer, she is the nurturer
She owns the light, the more she faces the darker
She cribs, she falls down the stairs
Thousands of pain she alone bears

She cries in the darkest nights
In the lonely streets she struggles with the fights
She holds the space and path for others
No matter how her inner world shudders

An awakened woman is a treat to be with
She creates the truth and breaks the myth
She does not entertain the lies and mongers
She burns the iron and fills the treasures

She breaks the cage and grabs the key
She spreads the love and negates the envy
Balancing all the scales of her life
She belittles the worries and takes a jive

She is the river, she is the ocean
She is the belief, she is the notion
She faces the mirror, she adores her beauty
She manages the chores, she performs the duty.

She mingles with the opponents
She plays with the fire
She is the Shakti, we should admire
She entices with her strength and inner fire

She is the matchless maiden
She passes the tests and unleashes the burden.
She struggles to be on the top,

She is the trust, she is the hope.

She weaves a story, she plays the tunes
She envelopes the mud, she bestows the dunes
She stems the happiness, she borrows the tears
She passes the storms, she holds the gears

She believes in the miracles
She solves every problem which she tackles
She raises toast to other women
When she becomes kali, she kills the demons.

She is the sunrise, she encompasses the storm,
She is an awakened woman, don't consider her a norm.

Poem By Rojalin Mahapatro

These Womens

These strong and delicate womens
Blue as the tint of concurrent lake,
Shone and foretelling the timeless light,
Swift as the purple night,

Swift as a touch, with a little head
Sprang with her wealth of social joy,
Resist attack, her youth to skill,
Pale flowers kindle with the bee,

Pale life, with her fields of summer,
Pale flowers kindle with my pretty hands,
Fair and golden as the moon,
Hold the judge with your regrets;

She felt as if a held assault,
She beheld them battling for the rush,
She bent behind my sails,
Brightly turned the fair lady wide and warm.

May day on the world by night,
She'd put the water true;
Swift as the snow the purple traffic
Then off she flew up to the same room,
High in the magic of love's youth;

You are the proper and a crown,
Lined with strong array, in which he took
Appeared a color of her name,
Shone and sang them with a name,
Transmute the first day of your human vision;

These strong and delicate womens
Shone and had shine,
Bow'd down thine head
To find doth in her face

A narrow stare,
Fresh was her rule,
She bent to find
Light of itself.

Rear'd this new throne,
Cold and soon gone,
Pale as the white,
Eyes look so far?

Fell out like flame,
Pink, small, and blue,
Gripping the rest,
As flakes of snow.

Saw a royal queen,
Keep the dark hair,
Sway'd the fair soul,
Sweet was her place.

Swaying her lips,
Rose and made sound
Spread her light shade
Where's yet the end?

Then quiver down,
Black drawn and gray,
Grey set it's teeth,

What's a keen sense?
Wherein she nought
Heard no day her,
Black as the sea
Filled with flame.

Short Stories By Shruti Sinha

From A Co-Ed School To An All Girls College

So like everybody else I was very young when I was put in this school by my parents. My father had made a list of few schools and he was very keen that I get an admission in one of those.

The junior branch of my school was located at Pusa Road, New Delhi. I still remember the first year of the school, it was a pathetic one. I made my father visit school on daily basis for whole one year. My teacher was so fed up with me. She advised my father not to visit daily otherwise I would never learn. Gradually I settled and made peace with managing alone.

I don't have many memories of my learnings in the junior school.

Then, in fourth grade, I moved to the elementary School in Rajinder Nagar. The senior branch was also there.

I am really grateful to my parents for putting me in a Co-ed School where boys and girls have mutual respect for one another; they are made to overcome the fear of the opposite gender by interacting more and more with them.

This Co-ed School was filled with competition, healthy competition. During my childhood, I never really saw any bias towards any gender in school. Both boys and girls were encouraged, motivated and were made to give their best in studies or sports or art.

One unnoticeable plus point of studying in a Co-ed school is also that you learn attachments and detachments very early in life. Believe it or not, this helps you deal with several aspects of a relationship, heartbreaks or broken friendships or true friendships, some real strong friendships.

I don't really have a bad memory from school.

The school was so fun. All the boys and girls would play together and tease each other. I noticed one really strong thing in the school, which was, these boys always encouraged girls and they believed girls could do a lot. There was unity, peace and harmony there. Sometimes if a boy encountered a problem, a girl in the class would say "stop worrying so much, I will help you out in sorting this." That time nobody knew really but these boys and girls were promoting equality in those days as well. Such instances would get me closer to humanity and make me believe in oneness.

Then in 2008, while I was finishing my schooling, I started filling admission forms in colleges. I never had any dream college. But I had one dream, to get an admission in some good college in "DU", University of Delhi.

I managed to get a seat In Daulat Ram College and Ramjas College, in North Campus. But I landed up in Maitreyi College, in South Campus at Chanakyapuri because a friend of mine had gotten an admission there. So I decided to join there. But I was pretty sure that I didn't want a "hons." course. So I picked up B.Com.

Although I wanted to study Economics or Math which I could easily have gotten in North Campus. But I didn't choose either of them. I chose my friend.

I had decided in my mind that in the coming three years, my education, pursuing B.com would be my second priority. And my primary motive would be to live these next three years of college, make friends, have night outs, skip lectures, mark proxy, enjoy each other's company and groom myself in college.

And I did all of these. I made the most amazing friends there. Friends for life, really.

What I really found interesting in the college was that girls from various regions of the country, of different communities had gathered in one classroom. That was fascinating.

So, unlike my school, I had gotten admission here on merit.

Undoubtedly I lived the best days of my life here.

One really beautiful thing I learnt about girls in the college was that "when girls compete, they compete."

But this was not it. These girls also believed in empowering each other by uplifting each other.

After spending one year in the college, I also got to hear many stories of young girls, of how they faced gender discrimination, or how they were ill-treated, or how they would get married off after graduating.

Here, I understood the meaning and need of women empowerment and gender equality.

There is a need to educate young girls, so, later they can decide what they want for themselves. To inspire them, to encourage them, so that after completing their graduation, they don't just get married off, rather they can work or continue with their education.

Focus has to be on gender equality as well which comprises of several measures, like equal right to education, right to equal pay at work and sharing of workload.

College really shapes you in becoming a better version of you.

Years ago, I made this decision of not pursuing a professional course and chose studying in this girl's college simply because I wanted to do that. And today, I could say, I made the right decision.

My college turned me into a woman of grace and substance.

I could say:

"I got to live the best of both worlds, a Co-ed school and an all-girls college."

2050, Realization Of Womanhood

Since ages we had been talking about how women had always got suppressed by men and women in their families, at workplaces or schools or colleges. Since 19th Century, we had been witnessing thousands or lakhs or numerous cases of female infanticide across the world. Earlier girls were not made to study or complete their education. They were not made to attend schools and colleges. Women were not allowed to work. They were restricted to their homes, slogging in the kitchen cooking for the male members in the family. Their life was never about themselves. They spent all their life for others.

Such had been the condition of women in the society.

Today, in 2050, those are the stories that seem, those had never existed.

Here in 2050, when a girl is born in a family, it is celebrated in the entire neighbourhood. Now a girl's parents no longer save a large amount of money for her wedding. Rather, now they have understood that it is more important for her to learn and grow. Girls are made to engage in Sports and fun adventurous activities. And this has been made a part of their curriculum in schools and colleges. Parents are now focusing on their daughter's education, interests and career development as much as their focus had always been on their son's. There is no difference left between the two.

At workplaces their is no disparity in the pay of a man and a woman. Both are respected, valued, and appreciated at work. Just like how women have the benefit of maternity leave, now even men have been granted a six month paternity leave, keeping in mind how important it is for men to spend time with their kids as well. And to help their wives during infant's growth and development.

Childbirth now has become optional, a matter of choice for women. It has become very common in every household. Women are not pressurised to give birth to a child by their in-laws or husbands or their own families. Their decision is very well respected and valued. Women are free to decide whether the want to give birth to a child biologicaly or opt for IVF or Surrogacy. They are completely understood if they don't even want to have a child.

Working in a job or running a business or becoming a caretaker to a child or an elder or simply not wanting to work and staying at home with their families or alone, all is encouraged and understood by the society. Wanting to depend on themselves or not having any problem in depending on a loved one, be that a mother or father or husband or anyone is very well understood and accepted. The balance between a male and a female seems so well that now men have also realised that it is not a big deal if the woman of the house earns and they stay back home.

Both males and females are accepting of each other, the way they are and how they feel. Both are open to each other, expressing themselves. Women no longer have to keep their emotions and thoughts to themselves.

Women are neither forced to get married or work after completing their education. This has become a matter of choice for them. Both men and women are appreciated if they choose to travel solo or pursue a hobby or simply live their lives the way they want.

Those women who choose to get married are not made to cook or look after their husbands and aren't even made to feel that they have to host dinners at home for the relatives. They are not made to feel that it is just theirs responsibility to look after the house.

So here in 2050, men and women are at par. Both are helping in each other's growth and development.

And most importantly, Women are loved by themselves.

Short Story By Vidya Premkumar

Wild Grass

Bang. That was the last sound she heard before she passed away. There was not much she could have done about that. She had been hit hard from behind with a kitchen pan. The violence of it had shocked her into momentary paralysis before she fell face down on the floor. After nearly an hour as her throbbing head came back to consciousness, she grimaced and tried moving. Her head felt too heavy and she flopped back on the floor. She lay there tracing all the events that led to this moment, the pool of blood under her, holding them in it.

****

Aleta had a peculiar name, especially for an Indian. Her mother wanted her to be unique and so named her something that was not heard of in India. She stood out because of her name. Otherwise she was a plain girl by 'normal' standards. She had no outstanding feature or qualities or capabilities. The only thing noticeable was the name . But after the initial curiosity about the name people soon lost interest in that soon. This did not seem to bother her much. She was a very happy child. She enjoyed her plainness. It upset her mother to no end that her daughter did not seem to have any ambition of grandeur. She would coax Aleta to try out different things hoping that something would catch her fancy.

So Aleta learnt a little bit of everything: piano, guitar, classical music, Bharathnatyam, Kuchipudi, tennis, chess, calligraphy, sketching, landscape painting and even ballet. She moved from activity to another in a few months without excelling at anything. After she turned 10 her mother gave up and let her be. She sighed and decided to concentrate on her other child who was 2 years old and seemed to be already good with maths. He showed a definite liking for numbers.

Aleta felt a rare freedom when her mother stopped concentrating on her and she enjoyed just doing nothing. She went to school and did her homework and also helped out her mother in the kitchen, but beyond that she did not feel the need to do anything with her life. She was not even interested in the happenings on social media unlike other kids of her age. Aleta would just lie in the bed watching the fan's blade move slowly. It gave her immense pleasure to just watch it go in circles without a beginning or an end. Even in winter she would turn the fan on and put it on the lowest mode because she could not sleep without watching it turn.

Her undemanding life pulled people who were restless towards her. She felt calming to such souls. As she grew up her being took on a peacefulness that radiated from afar. She seemed to be always looking inwards even when walking through the college campus. Many wanted to touch this peacefulness and satiate their indescribable constant hunger for life and action. Alwyn was no different. From the moment he saw her in the college canteen sitting by herself watching the table fan with intent and lost to the world, he felt he needed to know her and if possible absorb some of the peace she emanated.

When he rapped on the table she was sitting at, Aleta slowly pulled herself out of the reverie that she was in and looked at him half dazed. He repeated his question which he was now sure she had not heard, "Are you free to talk?"

"Huh? Do I know you?"

"No you don't. I am Alwyn, final year B.A. Sociology… You are a fresher right?"

"Yes. I am also in Arts. Division B."

"Ah, Psychology-History-Economics combination right?"

"Yeah." She looked at him for a little while as he squirmed under her honest wide eyed scrutiny. She wondered what he wanted as clearly even their subjects didn't match. "Ehm! You wanted to say something to me?"

"Ah, that! Well I don't really know but I felt I needed to talk to you.It is kind of absurd. But that is the fact."

"Oh ok. Well if you don't have anything really important to say to me can I have my table back?"

"That's rude.

"No, I think it is rude to disturb somebody you don't know when you don't really have anything to say."

"I do want to get to know you."

"Maybe some other time. Today I am not up to it. I would like to be by myself."

Alwyn felt challenged and though he did not show his displeasure on his face, the way he scraped the seat back to the table indicated it. She turned her eyes away from him and looked out of the window at the tall grass growing in the untended ground. He left under an angry cloud.

After that first not-so-pleasant encounter Alwyn began chasing Aleta with a vigour which went with his general attitude towards life. He thought of himself as a tiger who needed to hunt life and subdue it. Aleta placid response to all his overtures made him want to possess her even more. The more he pursued her the more did Aleta feel alienated from him. His overtures felt like the same pressure she had felt when her mother had pushed her into a spree of activities in her childhood. She could not explain that to him. He took her 'no' as personal failure and wanted to score a victory. But he didn't have much time as it was his final year and he needed to get a job before the end of the last semester.

****

Alwyn was proving a point at home also. His parents had wanted him to take commerce when his percentage had dropped in tenth. But he chose to pursue Arts. He told them about it only after securing the admission and by then it was already late for changing faculties. Alwyn told his parents that he would do well in this stream and get a good job. They were skeptical. Alwyn was just an average student and he was not short listed for the campus interviews and so many of the girls from his class already had job offers and he was struggling to find one.

Aleta's rejection of him hit him harder and he was trying to win her over to prove to himself that at least in relationship he can score. Alwyn was a good looking boy with definite charms that pulled most of the girls in the Arts stream towards him. Arts always had so few boys that the once who took arts were instant hit in the class with girls pursuing them and willing to do their homework, complete their journals and write or send pdfs of notes to them. Most of these guys developed a bloated ego by the end of the graduation. Alwyn was no less, especially with his good looks he had a bigger fan following. He could not believe that Aleta was not attracted to him. Facing failures on both fronts was hard on Alwyn. He was at his tether ends. His parents looked at him with disappointment and Aleta did not seem to care about his very existence.

****

Her curly hair tied up in a messy bun, the red house gown she had not changed in two days, the think green clinking bangles on her hand, Aleta took in her appearance in the mirror. She has had no time to do anything about them. Most of the bangles had slight crack, the gown was stinking with her sweat and carried stains of the food she had made for the last two days, and the hair had not been combed since two days and she had put on so much weight.. Aleta stood in front of the mirror on an old wooden cupboard and stared at herself while stuffing her mouth with buns slathered in butter. Where did she disappear in all that fats? Would she ever find herself again? Questions ran amok in her mind. After a long time she registered Alwyn's loud snores as he slept blissful of her turmoil in the dark room. She turned towards his shadow in the darker part of the room and then quietly walked out of the room and closed the door behind her.

Aleta made a cup of coffee in the dingy kitchen which was partitioned from the living room with a thin cardboard wall. She could hear his snoring through the door as she sat down on the settee that doubled up as the guest bed whenever her mother came visiting. She was the only one willing to come. His parents had refused to even look at her when they had a registered marriage and came home. They were not angry at her but they were angry that Alwyn decided to marry Aleta without a job on hand. They refused to support him. Alwyn still went ahead and got married to Aleta. Through all this Aleta had felt nothing.

As she sat sipping her coffee, images of Alwyn forcing himself on her in the wild grasses in the college ground flashed and she almost choked on her coffee. She had felt too numb to react when he had pulled her jeans down and roughly pushed himself inside her. The searing pain had knocked her unconscious. Late in the evening she had woken up, her body aching and to the voice of Alwyn.

"Now at least will you marry me? Nobody will touch you now when they know the truth about what happened to you. I am the only one you can marry." She wanted to scream and tell the world what happened to her but her mother had silenced her. When her mother heard about what had happened she had told her, "Think of it as a blessing that he is willing to marry you."

The apathy of her mother had completely shut her down. She mutely accepted her mother's insistence that she marry Alwyn. Right before the marriage she badge to eat tremendous amounts of food. She was constantly hungry. She now kept filling the void she felt with food. She became obese in just a few months. Nobody recognised her. She stopped caring for herself. Alwyn married her and took her home. She mutely followed him. His parents could not accept that he married a girl who had no qualities that could redeem her and he had done it without himself having a job. Alwyn had hopped from one temporary job to another and could not even hold down a position because he inevitably got into fights with the employers and would walk out of a job in anger. This cycle was never ending.

After the marriage he never touched her as he found her ugly and she was relieved. Every time he passed by her, her body involuntarily trembled. She tried hiding it but he felt it sometimes and looked angrily at her. Those nights he would come home drunk and beat her up. She would not even utter a sound and that infuriated him even further and he would continue his thrashing till he was exhausted and then slept it off.

Days and nights spun into a blanket I deliberate ignorance and Aleta stayed cocooned in it.

****

Wild grass. She stood on the same spot. There were still wild grasses around. The college still did not care to clear it up. Nobody really came there except for the furtive rendezvous of lovers who had no place to go. Four years. She still felt the chill run through her spine. She could not forget it. She had hoped it would fade with time. The memory. But it stayed sharp like a freshly sharpened knife, gleaming in the sun. She shuddered before turning away from that place and looking at a distance.

She visited that spot every year on the same day that she was raped. She hoped to feel something different. It was a weird kind of pilgrimage for her. She came to the spot praying that she would finally heal from it. Her mind screamed and willed the spot to help her for it was the mute witness to what happened to her. Four years and the spot made her feel the same.

Aleta returned the fifth year also. She was still the same, unkempt, overweight and dazed. As she stood on that ground and the evening turned dark blue, another figure appeared besides her and she turned to look at that person. A young girl who could not be more than 18 was standing there and seemed lost.

Aleta stole another glance at her and then stood in silence, sharing the space with that girl who had tears running down like a river deep in a mountain. Quiet from a distance. The girl turned to Aleta after a long time and asked, "You too?"

Aleta nodded.

"Will it ever be better?"

Aleta nodded her head in negative.

The girl digested that piece of information and again asked, "Did you even try?"

Aleta nodded her head in negative again.

"Why?"

"What's the use? They will say I asked for it because I refused him so much. Girls should not be such proud beings. She deserved it. My mother thought that way too. She named me Aleta and wanted me to be unique but ultimately she wanted me to just be like everyone else. What is the use of trying?"

"How do you know what would have happened if you had tried? I am trying even though it is not easy. Maybe you could now. It is not that bad when you try, you know."

Aleta watched that girl leave and continued to stay there. This is the first time that she spent so much time at that place from where her nightmares began. As she stood there contemplating, it occurred to her that she never even tried to say something awhen things happened to her. Maybe like that girl said maybe she could try.

****

That night when she got home Alwyn was drunk again. He bang his verbal abuse as he continued to down another bottle of liquor at home. It always began as that. But on this day, something had snapped in Aleta. She walked up to the door of the small bedroom where her husband was and quickly pulled the doors shut and bolted it from outside. Alwyn got really mad then and began banging on the door. He threatened to kill her when he came out. Aleta did not budge. She waited for him to fall asleep before opening the door. She went back to the kitchen and started cooking dinner.

Alwyn woke up in a rage. He saw the door open and rushed out still under the influence of the alcohol. He staggered to the kitchen, ready to bash up Aleta. Aleta coolly picked up the frying pan she had kept by her side and turned around and swung it with a perfect aim at his head. He crumbled and collapsed.

"Don't you ever raise a finger on me. Ever.", she said very calmly. "Next time you may not wake up in bed alive. I am leaving and don't dare to follow me or try finding me."

She calmly went into the bedroom and packed all the things she needed in a small suitcase and walked out of the flat. Alwyn sat in the kitchen still clutching his throbbing head.

Short Story By Sristi Sengupta

The Piecing

"I'm waiting for a train."

"Sure not here in London – not anywhere near Cotswolds even! Where are you?" Maggie made sure she sounds as worried as she can, you know how sisters are.

"Amsterdam."

"ON. NEW. YEAR'S. EVE?" no, no, she is furious.

"Is that all that's bumming your mood?"

"What do you mean?" she mumbled.

"I was in Winchester last night, tonight in Amsterdam. I haven't been home," my facts rolled off like beads from an unfastened string.

"That has me worried as well," her voice shivered.

"I don't have my passport, Mag, there are people after me and I can't hide in this booth for too long," I hung up. I know she is bothered too little about my errands and frisky truly when I say I'm in the mood for some Barrowboy and Banker's. She's my little sister, my cat, my purplish little Magpie. Little things matter to her, like walking with me through Piccadilly square on New Year's Eve. "She could go with her friends," I think to myself, "I'm the butt of an old brother, for god's sakes, she'll be fine!"

The uncomplaining Italian gentleman in a rustic brown suit with a bluish lining, standing in grave attention disguised like an old telephone booth, hiding me in his heart like a passionate revenge is startled by the shaking ground. I push his vest pocket open to peep outside. There it is the 8 p.m. train to Harlingen.

People are gathered at the front of the coach, I'm assuming they are returning from a party, quite an early leave I must say. Harlingen is seven stations far from here, if they aren't getting off anywhere in between then my mind will have something else for respite from tallying my chances of being deported back to London. These people, they maybe a family, five of them are sporting fiery red corals for heads – two girls and three boys. One of the boys is a little older than the rest, I can tell because he is clean shaved while the other two are somewhat conscious with their boyish beards all the way down to their necks – unmindfully scratching them in the middle of the jostling banter. The older one, on the contrary, mindfully stroking his cheeks with the back of his fingers but not as frequently - I can tell he is older because his need to look younger is exceeding.

Another is a woman, seldom partaking in the conversation, smiling nonetheless. Her cheeks are blushing like embers pressed under a copper kettle. Beside her is a black sachet of wool with a tiny person inside, standing at a distance in shiny black boots.

My gaze is fixed at this figure. I'm watching its pair of marble-white hands slowly lift up a pendant from under the muffler. Paper-thin fingers press the silver heart open and inside, the picture of an older gentleman. The hands bring the pendant closer to the hidden face and in the next moment I knew *she* kissed it, with a jolt the train started and the woman beside her said, "Emily, you know he's always with us."

Watching her touch the delicate metal piece to her lips reminded me of a similar possession – a piecing, a story, a memory. All that I have been through, over the last week, is for this little piece of engraved brass.

"Lange" carved in distant alphabets and then an uneven punch-hole – this set of nuisance on a tattered plate of brass no bigger than a finger tip had managed to turn my entire life into frenzy.

The last time I met Maggie, she'd naively tried to unravel a paradox, "Ernie, would you still think that we are doing things the right way?"

"What things?" I asked her, "What ways?" I added.

"You see, the older we grow, the newer our world gets," she put it like you put blueberry muffins in the oven for baking, without mittens but cautiously. I remember the book she was reading, Cold Mountain by Charles Fraizer. Triggered by the thought that the world might know where it's going yet unaware of what comes in the way, I interrupted her reading. We jokingly spoke about the world ending which trickled down to making notes on unfinished business, and then we thought about ringing up a few relations, cousins actually, who were great friends in our childhood.

That's when I was reminded of Grandaunt Maud.

"Maggie, do you remember Granma Maud?" I'd asked her in as little hope of affirmation as greater the trance of my memory grew. Of course she didn't, she had never even met this robust shelduck of a woman who carried herself like a doe on the feet of an otter. "Ze audazity!" she would snarl at the news-paper boy for throwing our bundle off the porch hitting and tipping the empty milk bottles over. This didn't happen too often since she wouldn't stay over at night unless mother said she was making stamppot. "Ye think ye mash zem well? Ze potatoes lumpier than ze zkin on my hands!" she would take away the piping hot bowl of soft potatoes from mother and start mashing them.

She loved her nephews. I'd know for I've seen her sneak up money into the pockets of forty year old, grown men, then pressing a haughty finger up to her lips, chuckling and bidding them not to tell their wives. We lived together in Terschelling, an island town in the Netherlands - father, mother and I, and Uncle Mason, and uncle Abbe with Aunt Julia.

"You would've loved being there, with family", I looked at Maggie with glistening eyes. "What about Grandma Maud? Where did she live?" Maggie asked curiously. "Oh, she travelled!" I said in juvenile surprise as if I was five again.

I never really had the chance to speak with my grandaunt, never did we chat about her encounter with the fairy people of Paris who flew all the way up to light the top of the tower or the gnomes in the vineyards of Italy who crushed grapes at midnight. We didn't because she wasn't somebody who would like to keep up the good spirit of a childish secret, not a great believer of magic perhaps, for children can sense sharp things faster than any grown up and stay away on their own if their little bubble is at risk.

But she was very sweet. She had a hard time smiling but her face didn't have a perpetual grimace. I poured in all that I remember of my childhood in Terschelling, in our old house and about Maud, "that's all – then Mum had you, and we decided it was best to come to London," I said to Maggie. "Hasn't father been here for a long time as well? I mean - ," she asked. "Correct, he came to London – to put up at the school in Winchester, he was only five, just three years after the war ended!"

Our father passed away in the summer of 1996. We woke up to him in his bed, sleeping too soundly to be woken up before the next lifetime. I never liked letting his memory pass without a visit to the kindness, love and care he carried in him everywhere he went. Therefore I got up to look for the memoirs I had of him. Maggie had one of mum's dearest possessions – an umbrella she'd inherited from her own mother. It was inoperable, to start with, but its embroidered fabric was still intact and the lace frills at the edge were regal. From father, I had collected a watch with a sun dial and a coin that he said had tipped off from Roosevelt's coat!

I love looking at the watch under the winter sun that moves swiftly across the sky, so does Maggie. I was fetching it from the drawer when I noticed the tarnished little piece of metal.

The sight of it flung me off to my past, the day we were leaving Terschelling, Maud had only come over for an hour or two and without enough words to suffice my remembrance now, pushed the little tablet inside my closed palm, then left. But what I have of it with me is only one halve.

I was curious about its origin; I supposed it was some kind of a ticket and upon some enlightenment from a local antique collector it wasn't a surprise that I had, unknowingly, caused the piecing of an identity. It was a child's name tag from an air raid identity bracelet. The last name was Lange. I was assured that it was a rare find since only six have been found in tact, unharmed. I was told post a closer look at the imprint that it might've been issued in Holland.

It was of course wild optimism to ring up our old house in hopes of catching up with someone close to grandaunt Maud, to shed some light on this artefact.

The new tenants picked up and said they had no clue. The only answer they had to my scattered questions was the possibility of an old woman, living all by herself, somewhere in Belgium with the name of

Maud Meyer. She would often require psychiatric assistance from the hospital since there was no one to keep her in good care besides professional care givers. My heart shattered. But before I could thank them for their help and bid a night I realized that our hearts can, at times, even disappear. They asked me how I was able to call the house to which I replied with my diligent record of having inhabited it. "I don't remember a co-tenant," the middle-aged, masculine voice scoffed. "I lived there as a child. It was my grandparents' house," I stated politely. There was muffled silence for a minute or two and in the background I could hear the man inquire, "Ma! Hadden de gebroeders Meyer kinderen? (Did the Meyer brothers have any children?)"

It was a bleak answer. I didn't hear it from his mother.

"Mason never married, Abbe never had kids. Please don't call us again."

"Please! I know, but their younger brother, Dan, did."

"They were two brothers, never heard of a third one. Good night, sir."

The man bore distant relations with my Grandma's sister. It was possible that the man was a nuisance. To him, so was I.

What I was trying to hold back in my eyes – confusion, abandonment and fear – escaped down my pallid cheeks in thin streams of loneliness when the train stopped with a jolt. It had reached Harlingen.

I checked in at a motel down town, placed coyly upon a drivers' pub.

When lying down on the bed didn't work I tried shutting my eyes and letting my brows to rest. I can't sleep. Every time my mind is taking charge it's reminding me of my desperate rummaging through phone directories, call records, letters, yearbooks and what not. On my last visit to Winchester, at the Mont Dell School for boys - where I knew my father had graduated from, the year books had no trace of a Dan Meyer! I begged the administrator for some sort of a record, a name, a hint, anything! Even showing his pictures didn't help until when I was soaked up in fatigue and anxiety; the lady looked over her high chestnut desk and said, "We keep our special admissions very discrete."

I am standing by the memorial hall at the foot of a gigantic fortification where one of the greatest German bunker and radar installations were run – witnessing the brilliant difference between the living and the lifeless, whilst martyrdom is a glory to buried bones it is a curse to concrete that is still above ground. I am no less lonely, starved or unwelcome than the building. I barely had luck getting help in deciphering the mystery of this name tag and my guts tell me I cannot go any longer. I turned back, like we all do.

"Hello, sir," said the sixty-something-man in a blunt brown suit, "Haven't we met before?"

"At the antique shop - back in Amsterdam, you were with the officers, I suppose?"

"Are they after you?" he chuckles, "I heard you asking around about Maud. She's an old pal to me Pop! I'm pleased to know there's somebody she can call her own." "If only I could see her!" I broke down in despair.

"Pick yourself up; it's a long way to go!"

"What do you mean?" I asked. "My son works in Belgium. He's called in a fax that'll do for your passport and about the other things, he will sort them out like a caring host," he smiled at me. "You'll take me there, to my Granma Maud?" I beamed like a child.

"Oh yes, yes! But I doubt if she still remembers you. Something's not right in her head."

"I'll keep that in mind, sir, but I don't know your name yet."

"Bram Smith," said Mr. Smith.

I am now in the lobby of a dainty, red house, asked by Mrs. Weber to wait until Granma wakes up. I slowly creep in after an hour into the room that's colder than the November rain.

"Who iz id?"

"It's me, Ernie – your brother, Willem's son."

"Broder? I haf no broder. Ged oud of here, now!"

"Granma Maud! Please!"

"Maud? Maud is dead! I am not Maud."

In a long time, I hadn't looked at her. Besides the three decades I hadn't even looked at her when I came in. She was Maud. She had to be Maud!

I sat down without a word. "Who are you, then?" I asked

"A voman. Can't you dell?" she hissed.

"But your name?"

"Don't they deach you in hisdory books?"

"Haven't read that one. Do you know Maud?"

"She lived vid me, in dis 'ouse."

"What happened to her?"

"One day she didn'd come bag. Like ze mosd of uz," she sighed.

"What do you mean?"

"You don't live vorever! Vich book did ye read aboud her?"

"She is my grandaunt, I think."

I am met with silence again. She hasn't spoken for ten minutes now. My senses are held back by the air raddled with lavender soap, spirit and cough syrup.

"Dey don't dell you aboud us," she started as if in a trance "because we are vemen. Not the only voman, but just vemen - very common. Dey don't haf our name in ze books. But ve haf seen ze Nazis march in like ze men haf. And ve haf stood our ground like dem. Ve haf shot gunz like dem – hand grenades, bombs and rifles - we haf fought. We haf protected like men protect and feared like men fear. But -," she stopped. "Id iz all gone now. Long gone. I don't vant to remember id," she finished speaking.

I don't want to remind her either. Mrs. Weber has come in to draw the curtains to keep the afternoon sun out. "I should get going," I must make sure that it's not selfish of me, "thank you for having me here, today." I am on my way out of her room but something catches the corner of my eye. Over the small hearth of the dormant fireplace, a miniscule white frame with the picture of two people - Granma Maud and a boy, seven or eight. "Ma'am," I said, "Anna," she stated. "Anna, who's this?" I asked. "Dat iz Maud wid her son, Dan," she answered. "Granma has a son?" I asked in shock.

Anna looked at me with her watery eyes, hazel and merciful, "had," she replied, "Her man, he vas in ze army. Ven ze Nazis came dey dook him in. Dey started daking efferybody, killing men, vemen, children. We dezided to fight bag. We didn't last the virst nighd. Dey dook my broder, Betty's husband, dey burn'd down the Miller's 'ouse and den, dey shot Dan, infrond of hiz moder. It vas dat bastard, Klaus, I remember because -," she stopped again and starred at me. "I remember because the night we bombed his barrack his boy was dere too and poor Maud, she dook ze boy away from his father! She said he vas innocend, she saved his life."

"What was his name?"

"Klaus Lange's boy - Hans! Hans Lange."

I am wondering if this is enough information for me to discover the truth at my own pace. But a lump in my throat suggests the truth isn't mine at all, it was hers to tell, my Granma Maud's. I have clutched my hands together and now ask Anna with whatever courage is left in me, "do you know what happened to Hans?"

"When I zaw her ze next time, Maud zaid dat ze boy remembers noding, she has kept him ad her broder's 'ouse, in Terschelling."

Short Story By
Priyanka Joshi - More

The So-Called 'Perfect' Marriage

"Vishakha Singh, will you marry me?" he asked me, down on one knee.

"Oh my god! Yes!"

I had dreamt of this day, ever since I met Rahul. We met at a business conference that I attended with my boss. It was love at first sight. He was rich, he was attractive and good-looking, he was popular and he loved me… what more could a girl ask for? Ever since then whenever we had the chance, we would meet for dinner if he was in my city or I travelled to meet him, and even took vacations together. Last night he called me up as he had come to my city and we planned to meet tonight for dinner, but the proposal was a surprise.

We announced it to our families after we met them. First, we went to my hometown and then we went to his. A grand wedding was planned with an expensive wedding planner. The wedding attire for us for all the functions and jewellery was designed by top designers personally. No stone was left unturned as Rahul Makhija, CEO of a top company was getting married. Our wedding was covered by the press as we had celebrities attending the wedding. He was truly one of the eligible bachelors, and he was mine!

In a grand affair, we were married. We had our honeymoon on a cruise liner. Life could not be any better than this. I left my job in the previous city and moved to Rahul's city but I did not take another job here as now it was not required. There was nothing more that I could ask for. I had everything. All I needed to do was give him my time and love.

Being Rahul Makhija's wife felt nothing less than a celebrity. He had friends who were politicians, film stars, industrialists and there was always some event or party, function, a conference or so that we had to attend, in a week. Rahul always ensured I wore and carried branded and designer clothes and accessories. My wardrobe was full of it, and I loved it.

I made friends with some of his friends' wives. Some of them were social workers who owned NGOs, some film actresses, who had either married film actors or businessmen while others were into their own business or housewives. Of all of them, I made two close friends, Priya, who was an actress before her marriage to an industrialist and now designed shoes, traveled frequently to world destinations for work and Mitali, a housewife who was a lawyer but left the practice.

Rahul would often be busy in his meetings and work, so there were times when I stayed alone for days. When I was his girlfriend, at least when we were together, he was only mine at that time but now when we belong to each other, he has become less available. I explained to myself that now he was mine forever and always spending time together was not essential. I had to learn to adjust and understand that I was the wife of a businessman and they are not always available for their family. He gradually became busier on his business trips, asking me to attend events and invitations alone, representing him or on his behalf. At times, I felt lost just going to social events all alone. When I mentioned this to Rahul over the phone, he brushed away the topic. When I told him that I missed spending time with him, he suggested that I could keep myself occupied in many ways - like attending events such as art shows and conferences, shopping, reading, socializing with friends, gyming, or helping out in some NGO.

'You will get used to it,' Mitali remarked when I told her about what Rahul had said. I looked at her confused. Mitali mentioned that initially she too felt lonely, as she had given up her career and missed working and her husband was unavailable after months of their marriage. Mitali belonged to a family of lawyers but still, she had given up her practice as her husband did not like it. She explained to me that initially, I would mind it but with time I would learn to accept and live with it. That night I pondered upon what Mitali said. At the time of our marriage, I knew what I was getting into, but somehow it was now when reality struck that made me actually realize what I was - I had become a showpiece wife. I was not happy with my identity and I had to change this.

The next month when I knew Rahul was returning from one of his trips, I decided to surprise him with a candlelight dinner. I laid rose petals on the floor making a heart. I also sprinkled some petals on the bed so as to make it more romantic. I cooked all his favourite dishes. His flight was scheduled to arrive at 8 p.m., which meant he would be home by 10. I had also asked the cook and other servants to leave, so it was personal. He arrived a little later than 10 and was surprised to see the decorations and preparations.

'What's all this,' he asked in amazement.

"Surprise for you, we hardly get to spend time together so I decided we do tonight," I replied taking off his coat.

'Someone seems to be in a very romantic mood', he commented turning around to face me smiling. I nodded.

"Let's eat, I've made your favourite dishes", I replied holding his hand pulling him to the table. He sat and I sat next to him. As we ate, he asked me what I was up to lately, to which I mentioned the places and events I had visited which I could think of.

"Enough about me, what about you?" I asked him as he had returned after weeks.

He told me about the places he went, the people he met and meetings he had attended. Although uninteresting, I paid interest as in marriage, each spouse has to be a good listener. Also, as I was his wife, it was my duty to take interest in his business matters. Our conversation was interrupted when Rahul's phone rang. He went inside to attend the call while I sat at the table finishing my dinner. After dinner, we walked into our bedroom and he saw the scattered rose petals on the bed.

'Sorry but I am really tired tonight, babe,' he said.

"Rahul, it's been so many days, I have missed you so much, please, Honey," I insisted. I began to caress him and stroke his hair, trying to lure him but he gently pulled my hands away and shook his head. I could feel a gush of frustration but controlling myself, I said, "Ok we will do this some other time, not tonight, important thing is you are back so we have the coming days ahead."

'I have to leave next week for Canada, important work,' he said brushing the petals, sitting on the bed looking at his mobile.

"But why? you just came!" I said in a raised voice.

'It's for work Vishakha. I am not enjoying on vacations!'

"Yes, I get it but don't you want to spend time with me? I am your wife, consider me when you make plans."

'What do you expect? I just shut the business and spend all my time with you?'

"I expect that you spend 'some' time with. I am alone at home for days, trying to spend time, without you, doing things I do not enjoy."

'What do you not enjoy? You have always enjoyed shopping, travelling and socializing. So how is it any different from what you did before marriage that you do now?' he stated in an irritated tone. His phone vibrated but he ignored it, eventually switching it off.

"I am your wife now and I want to spend time with you, not others. I feel lonely in such a big house. I keep calling my friends over for company, but they cannot suffice your absence," I tried explaining. He lay and turned to the other side. The night was ruined. I decided to lie down also. As I lay there, I kept thinking to myself, why Rahul failed to understand my loneliness. He had just come and now and he was insisting on going back again. Why did he never consider my feelings? Busy in thoughts, tired from the cooking and preparations all day, I dozed off to sleep.

The next morning, I was awakened by a phone call. I answered it without looking at the number, it was Mitali on the other side. She had called to inform that Priya had committed suicide. I sat up in shock, not believing my ears what she just mentioned.

"When and how?" I managed to utter in shock. She mentioned that it happened sometime yesterday, and as she was a former actress and a wife of an industrialist, police got involved instantly - is all Mitali knew. We decided to visit Priya's house to convey our condolences. As I cut the call, I shook Rahul to wake him up to give him the news. He asked me in a sleepy voice what the matter was, to which I informed about the sad news. His eyes opened wide and he sat up. 'This is terrible news,' he commented. I informed him that Mitali and I were going over, he could join us also. But he declined that he would meet Naveen (Priya's husband) afterwards.

When Mitali and I reached the place, media vans and police jeeps stood outside the gate. As we reached inside, Naveen was nowhere to be seen, but Mandira, Priya's teenage daughter was sitting on the couch, surrounded by people. She looked distressed, which was natural as she had just lost her mother and stiff, knees crouched to her chest, we went up to her and spoke trying to comfort her but she barely reacted. I went closer and gently stroked her hair, taking a strand behind her ears, "Dear, if you need anything, we are here for you." She lifted her eyes to look at me expressionless then looked away. Mitali was speaking in a low voice to the other people in the room. She signalled that we should leave and I gave Mandira a last look and walked out. When we got into the car, Mitali informed me what all she found out. Priya's body had been taken for post-mortem and tests while Naveen was at the police station being interrogated for what happened. Although there was a suicide note by Priya stating that she was committing suicide of her own will and no one was to be blamed for it, the police were uncertain as there were bruises on her body.

"Bruises?" I asked, stunned.

'Yes, so I heard, wonder what happened?' Mitali replied.

She dropped me home. As I entered and was walking over to the bedroom, Rahul who was in his study, came out asking me what happened. I narrated to him briefly what happened there and what I was told by Mitali. He placed his hand rubbing his forehead, 'This is really bad!' he remarked.

"I wonder what happened between Priya and Naveen. But I am more concerned about Mandira, poor girl, I feel terrible for her," I added. I walked to my room for a bath while Rahul stood there. As I showered, I could only think about how painful it must be for Mandira to lose her mother; what Priya had to endure at the hands of Naveen. If she was bruised, it was evident that he was violent with her. She needed to get justice. We had to wait for the final report from the police.

Two days passed since that day, and although I was deeply affected by Priya's death as she was a close friend, I resumed normalcy. That evening, I had an invitation to visit the opening of an art gallery. I asked Rahul if he would join me, but he refused that he had a meeting. He suggested I wear the new dress he bought for me from his recent trip along with the fine necklace that he brought to match with it. I complied. That night, when I returned, I tried to entice Rahul again, but he pulled away.

"Why are you doing this, are you not interested in me anymore?" I confronted him.

'Nothing like that, why have you become so eager all of a sudden?' he asked. I sighed.

"Rahul, I am alone all the days when you are out, so I thought maybe it was time we had kids now," I replied. His eyes widened, but not in joy as I had expected, in fact, it was more in shock.

'What are you saying? Kids? I thought we had decided we would not have kids. So why this all of a sudden.' He spoke nervously as he stood up. I explained to him that sooner or later we would be starting a family as we had agreed upon not having kids in the initial 5-6 years of marriage, but now we could. His business was stable, I was not pursuing a career and it was the right age also to become parents. But no matter what I explained he argued at each point and in the end, he just walked out of the room. It was clear that he did not want kids, I sat on my bed grieved at his reaction. I sobbed covering my face with my hands.

The next morning, at breakfast, Rahul and I ate in silence, when the doorbell rang. As one of the servants opened it, he came to inform us that there was a policeman at the door, seeking Rahul. Shocked to hear, I turned to Rahul who had frozen in fear. Reading his face, I felt suspicious. I immediately called our lawyer, who left to be on his way. We met the policeman, who introduced himself as an officer and stated that the purpose of the visit was to take Rahul to the police station, for some queries. He had all the documents. I assured Rahul that the advocate was on his way. I was on the way in the other car, when I received a call from an unknown number. As I answered it, the voice on the other side said, 'Hello Vishakha aunty, this is Mandira'. Surprised to get a call from her I asked her what she called for. She mentioned that she wanted to meet me.

"Right now?!" I asked I was on the way to the police station. She affirmed. So, I instructed the driver to turn towards the location she mentioned. When I reached the venue, she was there wearing huge sunglasses under a hoodie, covered from head to feet, barely recognizable.

"Why did you want to meet me here? You could have come home or I could have come to your place," I said walking towards her.

'I wanted to meet you in private, sorry for the inconvenience,' she replied. She gestured me to sit on a chair.

'Aunty, there is something I want to say to you, which is very disturbing but true and I think you should know about Mumma's death,' she spoke in a grievous manner. I looked at her stunned wondering at what she was about to say. What she said after that with visual pieces of evidence, left me horrified. I felt like the ground had slipped away from under my feet. Rahul was having an affair secretly with Priya, they went on business trips together and spent leisure time there. Naveen had uncovered it and that night, when Rahul and Priya had returned, Rahul came home to me, while Priya when she reached home, was confronted by Naveen. As their argument heated, Naveen ended up hitting Priya, bruising her body and face. Priya threw a fit screaming that she will leave the house, locked herself in the room but in the morning when the servant went to give her breakfast, she was discovered dead. Mandira had witnessed the events of the night and was aware of her mother's affair also.

Mandira ended by saying, 'Aunty, I am sorry to break this to you, but this is what happened. Also, I had seen Mumma's phone, the last call she made was to Rahul uncle, a total of 22 times.' She got up and walked away silently. I was so repulsed imagining what happened, I could not respond or react to her in any way. My shock was broken by the vibration of my phone in my handbag, it was a call. I answered it. It was the advocate on the other side calling me to come to the police station where they had Rahul as he was accused of being involved in Priya's murder. I took a deep breath and answered, "I am coming."

I reached the police station, where Rahul was behind bars. I walked up to him, he came closer, 'Look at this Honey, can you believe it? They think I am involved in Priya's suicide. I will get the best lawyers involved and get out of here.'

I looked at him and asked with a straight face, "When were you going to tell me that you had an affair with her?" He was dumbfounded. He could not refuse, as he realized I knew it all. I added, "It all adds up now, why you weren't interested in me, your so-called business trips and the fact that you wanted me to look like I was the perfect happy wife so that no one will ever doubt you of being involved with someone else." He remained silent.

I turned around to walk over to the officer, who began to assure me, 'Madam, we are only doing our job, your husband is a suspect as we have evidence against him, but if he is innocent, he will be free.' Instead, I surprised him when I requested to know what was the last conversation between the 'dead' (I was so disgusted by the truth that I could no longer call her by her name, she was no longer a friend) and my husband. He played the voice recording in which Priya and Rahul were clearly audible. She informed him that Naveen had discovered their affair and she wants to leave him and Rahul should leave me and come to her, so they can stay together. Rahul declined stating that she was only his interest, he did not want to ruin his image as the ideal husband and I was his showpiece wife. She threatened to kill herself, to which he replied that she was free to do whatever she desired but he will not budge and hung up. The officer stated that she possibly tried calling him till early morning, as per call records, after which she committed suicide. I stood up from the chair and sat on the bench nearby.

I recalled that night, Rahul had attended a call around the same time, he was also fidgeting with his mobile for a while, and then switched it off. I remembered the photos and videos Mandira showed me, the two of them together in hotel lobbies and at various locations. It was clear to me now, why Rahul was reluctant to have kids. He wanted to keep me as a showpiece, this perfect body figure, expensive clothes and accessories so that people assumed how great our marriage was. I was impressed by those first but gradually, the heavy price I had to pay emotionally and biologically to carry these expensive items and standard of living. Sitting on the bench, in the police station, my life flashed before me and I decided what had to be done. I got up and walked out of the police station, promising myself never to walk in there again, breaking all ties with those inside there too.

Short Story By Dipayan Chakrabarti

The Womb

One spring afternoon I met two beautiful women in the flower garden of our cottage who were sitting under a tree. "Say your names," I chirped. "I'm Urvasi and she is Menaka," one of them responded, pointing at the other woman sitting next to her. The woman who performed the introductions was tall and slim with bright vivacious manner. "We're *apsara*s," said the shorter of the two. "I mean celestial dancers." "Where do you live?" I asked, utterly baffled. Urvasi, the taller of the two replied, "In *Indraloka*." "Where?" I asked again, staring at the two women in disbelief. Both women smiled. "Are you really the famous celestial singers and dancers?" I queried. "Do you inhabit the heaven of the god Indra?" I asked in amazement. "Yeah, right!" answered Menaka.

"Would you care to join us on our journey?" Urvasi questioned, raven hair bouncing on her forehead as she walked towards me. I said, "Sure."

"O.K. fine," Urvasi said.

"What'll be the means of travel?" I asked.

Urvasi discussed something with Menaka. A few moments later, they gifted me with the ability to fly and to go back into the past. They also gifted me magical powers. Please follow us," Urvasi said.

***

The three of us moved through the air using the wings. We flew like birds; soaring across rivers, jungles, rice terraces, temples etc. We remained invisible. Nature ran past through wetlands and woodlands.

Shortly afterwards, Urvasi said in an edgy tone, "I'm worried about Princess Ujjaini." Menaka questioned, "Who is she?" Our wings flapped in the breeze. "Ujjaini is the unmarried princess of the kingdom of Avanti," Urvasi said. "She has a bun in the oven." "It means that she is pregnant," I reflected. "I think so," replied Urvasi. "Oh dear!" Menaka exclaimed.

"Can I know the story?" I questioned. "Who is the father of the unborn baby?" "One of the palace slaves," replied Urvasi. "The princess had told her father that she wanted to marry her lover." Menaka said, "It's a big slap on society too." "Yes, right!" Urvasi affirmed. "She looks confident." "What happened next?" I queried eagerly. "The lover was arrested and thrown into the prison," Urvasi replied. "A forced abortion may occur by order of the king."

"Men like to dominate," Menaka said. "The kingdom of Avanti appears to have no law that protects the freedom to choice one's spouse." "It appears so," Urvasi agreed.

"How did the princess react to the sentence?" I asked. "When she had heard this she found it impossible to speak; her eyes were filled with tears. But now she has to make a firm decision if she wants to keep the baby," Urvasi replied, waving her red wings. "Against her father's wishes, I guess," I assumed, bringing my hands up to shield the face in awe and wonder. "Oh, right" said Urvasi. "The princess is a very strong-willed woman." Menaka asked, "So, what is the task, *sakhi*?" "We've to rescue the embryo of the pregnant princess from abortion," Urvasi stated.

***

At last we reached the royal palace. We arrived indoors as the sun slowly sank below the horizon. Princess Ujjaini was sitting in her boudoir, surrounded by her maidservants. We got into her belly assuming tiny shapes.

***

We crept along the dank tunnel in the dimness. Wandering through blue farmlands, yellow hillocks, and red rivers, we finally hit an elevated region.
"Get some rest," said Urvasi. 'It's very draining." "Thank you!" I replied tiredly.

Urvasi looked tired from exhaustion. Menaka looked relieved as we stopped to rest. There was a vacant gaze in the eyes of the two *apsara*s as they stared at the wilderness. Shortly afterwards, we climbed up the rocky heights that promised a wide view, and on reaching the top, I was able to see the forest trees.

A few moments later, Urvasi gestured towards a stream which looped past the land. I listened to the soft bubbling sound of water. "Seems a bit creepy, isn't it?" I said to Urvasi. "Yeah, right," she replied. Menaka said, "I can't walk any further- I'm pooped."

A small hill with a flat top and steep sides popped up before the eyes. It was an area of outstanding natural beauty. Shaken by no wind, drenched by no showers, and invaded by no snows, the mound was set in a sea of air with a purple glow playing over all. I inhaled the air. Suddenly, a canopy of mauve clouds swept down on us from the sky. A wisp of smoke straggled up through the trees.

Menaka stood on the rocky floor, motionless and still, gazing absently. I saw a shallow cave-like opening at the base of the cliff. Trailing round the very mouth of the cavern, some bunches of wild berries hung temptingly. I walked towards the opening. The opening to the cavity was only a narrow hole between two rocks. We entered the cave redolent with a strange smell. It was pitch-dark inside the cavern. We decided to rest.

Getting out of the cave after a short time, we started our journey. After a few moments, we reached a flat terrain. The eerie howl of the wind sent shivers down my spine. A colourful display of indigo, blue, green, yellow, orange, and red streaks of light appeared to undulate like waves in front of our eyes. They rippled and danced, faded and reappeared again. I stared so hard that my eyes seemed about to pop out of my heads. Urvasi and Menaka stood there, bug

-eyed. I gazed upwards till my neck ached. I muttered, "I'm in something of a tizzy." Urvasi rolled her eyes. "Wow, that's incredible!" Maneka exclaimed.

Strong winds blew off in the thin atmosphere. After a short time, the wind died down. An uneasy calm prevailed in the area. Urvasi asked me, "Are you anxious?""No, not at all," I said. "I'm feeling good," Urvasi said, whistling a tune.

Despite the enthusiasm, I worried about the surroundings. Suddenly, more darkness fell upon the sleepy little land. A warm breeze sprang up. After a while, we resumed our journey.

In due course, we reached a river where red water was always bubbling up and swirling by. I gazed at the stream in awe and wonder. "My friends," said Urvasi, "wash clothes."Urvasi sang in a beautiful voice as she dropped the dirtiest clothes into the pool of water.

After bathing and rubbing ourselves with oil we ate blue food. We began our journey after a while. We flew across the strange land. Moments later, we descended upon a rocky hillock with blue trees.

We came across an opening after a while. It communicated above with a hollow and inverted pear-shaped structure with thick walls. It lay in a deep cavity between two structures. There was a small opening under the structures. It liaised with the grim tunnel we had crossed earlier. The pear-shaped form was attached to the wall by a double fold of natural garters.

Moments later, we entered the lean overlay. Urvasi guessed, "This may be the body of the main part of the womb of the princess. "Perhaps you're right," I said. We went inside to the upper corners. Two tube-like structures entered from the openings. Urvasi said, "I can see two clear ducts.""Let's move forward," Menaka said. We crawled towards a lump of flesh. "Is it the embryo?" I asked, rising my eyebrows. "I think so," said Urvasi. It looked healthy.

"It's hot and stuffy in this pit," Menaka grumbled after a while. I said, "Yeah, right.""Let's fly to the palace where the king indulges in rest during leisure time," Urvasi said.

***

Moments later, we got out of the womb of the princess and assumed normal shapes. We flew over the trees. Shortly afterwards, my gaze shifted, and I stared into the distance.

A sweet fruity aroma wafted through the air. I looked down from above. An orchard came into view after a while. A quiet contentment spread through me. Types of berries dangled from the trees. The orchard was flanked by two meadows. The fields were planted with citrus trees. A flock of birds flew past us.

We descended near the palace after a while where the king uses to indulge in rest during leisure time. From four separate springs four rivulets ran in many different directions. It was indeed a spot where even an immortal visitor must pause to gaze in wonder and delight.

"Who're you?" a man squeaked. The man was armed with a spear. His men moved into position. The sharp-pointed heads of the spears sparkled in the sun. I got goose bumps. "We've come from a far-off place," Menaka said. "We've come to take part in the dance competition," Urvasi said quickly. The leader of the group extended his right hand and gave a loud yell of indignation, "Permit?" Urvasi raised her index finger and brought it over her lips. I decided to keep quiet. Menaka stared at Urvasi, slack-jawed. The guards took us away.

***

We were locked up in a stinking cell. The prison cell dehumanized convicts and it appeared to me dens of corruption. The sexual abuse of young prisoners and caste discrimination were common. I observed that some prisoners were disallowed to drink water from some wells while others were allowed access to potable water. I saw that stripping, parading naked, and forced shit eating were quite common in the claustrophobic atmosphere of the prison.

One day the guards dragged an old man to an empty prison cell. A lyre hung via a baldric over his shoulder. He had an innocent expression on his face. He showed unmistakable signs of fear. "Are you a musician?" Menaka asked. "A busker to be precise. I got arrested while singing," he replied with doleful eyes. "Please sing us a song," I requested. He sang in a beautiful voice with lyre accompaniment. The cruel and unfair treatment of the people of the kingdom of Avanti was told through the song. "You've a euphonious voice! Urvasi exclaimed with her mouth open. A beatific expression appeared on Menaka's face as the song came to an end. I was unable to believe what I had heard. "It seems that no freedom of expression exist in the kingdom of Avanti. You cannot express your beliefs and attitudes," Urvasi reflected with sadness. Menaka said, "It appears so."*

One day Urvasi was sleeping in the lockup in an uncomfortable position. She woke up with a start when a guard turned the key and opened the prison-door. One of the guards brought a liquid having the appearance of soup. The stink turned my stomach. Menaka lay with her face towards me, in a very deep sleep, breathing slowly and heavily.

"What's up?" Urvasi asked when the security guards disappeared from view. "I'll deal with them, so don't get yourself in a sweat about it," Urvasi said.

Two of the guards came in the evening. Urvasi and Menaka had the power to charm. The two *apsara*s won the guards over with their smile, their glamour and their allure. Hypnotised by magic, the guards stood like pillars, motionless as if turned to stone.
Urvasi said, "Let's go." We moved past them.

***

By the time we came out of the prison, Menaka had reached. The sky looked like an overturned black wok of awesomeness. We reached the royal garden and the leisure pool of King Adityanarayana.

***

It was foggy and through the fog the lights of the mansion gleamed mysteriously. We crawled towards a lake under the cover of night and fog. King Adityanarayana stood at the foot of the stairs that went down to the pool. I felt strange seeing King Adityanarya as he stood on the stairs of the lake without any clothing. A bevy of beauties walked towards the pool, stark naked. They held lighted candles as they walked. The light of the candles gleamed through the fog. The king gave a playful push to the leading woman and she fell into the water.

"Oh no!" I exclaimed, "What a crazy thing to do!" Urvasi grimaced when she saw the kooky game. Menaka stared at the bizarre spectacle with a sombre expression. The king pushed the women from behind as they fell into the pool. They swam holding the lighted candles by thin sticks between the teeth. We watched as the flames were doused in water.

We flew above a lake with quick, fluttery wingbeats towards the other side "Hey, look over there,"

Menaka said suddenly. A giant statue of King Adityanarayna stood on a high platform, overlooking the lake.

***

"Take a look," pointed Urvasi. "The walls are also made of bronze." "Yeah, they are topped with marble tiles too," Menaka said. The walls extended on both sides of the area from the threshold to the back of the court. The interior of the well-built mansion was guarded by golden doors that hung from bars of silver which sprang from the bronze threshold. Some girls practised singing and dancing. Certain young girls prepared different perfumes and fragrances.

"We've reached the courtroom," Urvasi said in a low voice after a while. I fixed my eyes in a steady, intent look. All eyes fell on the two beautiful women as they came into the royal court-room. The hall gleamed with bronze, copper, gold, amber, silver, and ivory. It seemed to me that the lofty hall of King Adityanarayana was lit by something of the sun's splendour or the moon's.

"Are y'all goddesses or mortal women? Do you haunt the steep hill-tops, the springs of rivers, or the grassy meadows? Your beauty, grace, and stature remind me of the immortal gods!" the king said, shaking his head. "You ask us where we hail from. I will tell you. We've come from a far-off place to take part in the dance competition," Urvasi replied in a deep husky voice. Everyone paid careful attention to the conversation.

"Please get your art noticed," the king requested. Urvasi and Menaka danced with accompaniment of a lyre. I watched silently. The king had a smile on his face. "Excellent maidens!" the king exclaimed. "I don't know what to say."

"Thank you, sir." The king seemed very happy about the dance performance. As the dance ended, all spectators rose to their feet and applauded. Urvasi showed her interest in the king by outward signs and motions. It was just an act. The king tried to gain her over by various ways and means. "I want to meet you in the pleasure room," the king told Urvasi eagerly. Urvasi hesitated for a moment, and then agreed to the proposal. There was a faint hint of a smile on her face. A short and general silence followed. The silence was not a comfortable one, only becoming awkward as Urvasi reached the door of the pleasure room. Menaka stood gazing at her friend.

From outside, the gift of magic gave me a clear view of inside activity. Flowers, in shades of red, pink, orange, blue, and white raised the beauty. Urvasi welcomed the king with a smile. The king feasted his eyes on her beauty. He went and bathed in polished baths, and after the maidservants had washed him, rubbed him with oil and dressed him in cloaks and tunics, Urvasi took her place beside King Adityanarayana. The king seated himself on a golden chair while Urvasi laid at his side the various kinds of food and drink that mortal men consume. Then she sat down herself facing her royal admirer; some maids set some wine beside him, and the two helped themselves to the dainties spread before them. The king held her hand intentionally and sprinkled upon her the water brought for rinsing his mouth. "Get nearer, sweet maid," said the king. But Urvasi rose to standing position and walked away leaving the king stranded. The king became blind with a passion for lovemaking, and put his arms around her. He closed his eyes and tried to kiss the pretty *apsara*. Urvasi slipped a drug into the bowl in which their wine was mixed. The drug had the power of robbing virility of its sting. The tyrant was reduced to a mere soft flower and suddenly became unconscious. Finally, Urvasi stepped out of the room, oriented herself and walked toward us.

A terrible warfare broke over the embryo. We fought against King Adityanarayana and his troops to save the embryo. In the beginning, the royal army gave stiff resistance. So advantageous was the king's position and so well did he resist our attack that the royal soldiers still held their ground. A spasm of rage and anxiety seized me. The king raised his voice in a terrible shout and released a gleaming arrow from his bow. "Take that" he shouted. "It's always easy to brag when you are in a better position," yelled Urvasi as she hurled an explosive fizzy stew of energy at the king. As the weapon struck the king, he fled to the nearby forest. Without their leader, the royal army became hopelessly disorganised. We were quick to profit by the situation, and the royal force was compelled to retreat.

***

Shortly afterwards, we entered the boudoir of the princess where she looked like the cat that ate the canary. She smiled smugly, showing off her baby bump. It was an extension of her body. It breathed with her. It moved with her. Life was pretty tumultuous, and she couldn't run away from it. It got dark at nightfall, marking the end of the day.

***

Suddenly, a cool mountain breeze drifted in from the surrounding hills and touched my face. The images disappeared without a trace. I found myself sitting alone in the garden staring blankly into the distance.

Short Story By Juju's Pearls

"She Is Living A Miracle Called Life!"

Prologue

This story is doesn't revolve around a character who is superwoman or downtrodden or a woman who has been physically abused or is physically disabled etc. This story is our story, the story of every female who takes birth on this planet. This is about her daily challenges –small or big which she faces right from the time she is born, in her different growth stages, during her school life, college life, work place and marriage etc.

If one is honest about their individual experiences and share in the same spirit without add on, I believe this world would be a better place. The stigma of being judged is so deep rooted that majority of women don't come out in open to talk about the abuse they have experienced ,be it verbal, physical, mental, social or professional.

Our society is male dominated and females have often been portrayed as an object of desire and want. Very less is talked about them as being individuals or possessing their personality. She is considered as a subordinate to the male species in the highest evolved species on Mother Earth.

The world smells of hypocrisy. Women are worshipped during the day and the scenario changes as the day dawns. Majority of us will resonate with this story.

It's about us, our journey.

Story

Woman, finest creation of God, seems like God made her from his soul. Yet, human beings tend to question the Almighty by suppressing and oppressing her. Her physical attributes and emotional, nurturing nature has led to creation of wide gap. In the game of power play, the one with superior physical strength wins. Maybe this has led to the terms like, weaker sex, fairer sex, women empowerment and so on.

The whole concept of women empowerment seems a farce. First, you label womankind as less powerful and then play the philanthropic role of women empowerment. Who has given man the right to label or judge God's creation? As such it's more important for a woman to empower another woman. Then we don't need to rely on anyone. Since ages, a woman has been the toughest opponent of another woman. One can go down the pages of history to verify on this. A woman assumes various roles in a lifetime and is engulfed with insecurities in different decades. As a child, she has to strive for attention from parents and society at large to be able to get the recognition as a living being. Next decade brings about physical changes and she struggles with transition from childhood to adolescent. Further decades escalate to youth, womanhood and the associated responsibilities. All along she has women in her circle adorning different roles- mother, sister, grandmother, teacher, friend, house helper etc. Unknowingly, their behavior and approach towards life leaves a footprint in her memory. She becomes a summation of many such footprints. These act like her shield in challenging times.

Let's understand this by going through the story of one such XX genotype Joa, who stood the test of time and emerged as a winner. She shut the mouths of society and persons in her family. Joa is a normal girl who did ordinary things in extra ordinary ways which polished her and she turned into a priceless diamond. Each stage of her life is filled with stories of her courage, strength and ability to consider problems as situations and setbacks as opportunities.

The initial decade since Joa opened her eyes first was a smooth ride. As she entered her teens, she felt that the world around her had changed. Everyone started looking at her like an object. She could feel the infinite piercing eyes, which scanned her from top to bottom, left to right. She started feeling vulnerable. She had a great relation with her parents and she shared her fears. Her mother counseled her regarding the phase of entering teens, the physical changes which begin to occur in girls. Since, the growing girl becomes conscious of these changes, the feeling of being watched and judged comes as part of the package deal. Further, her mother suggested she enroll in self defense classes and join some sports activity which will make her physically strong and will help in alleviating these thoughts. Joa joined hockey in sports along with self defense classes. While traveling from home to school and to her evening classes, she held her hockey stick in her hand. She felt powerful and in control from within. She gained self confidence that she was armed and ready to face the world. One day while going home in a public transport, she didn't get a seat. As a result the obvious choice was to stand with support. After a while she felt something hard pressing behind her. She felt a pressure and moved forward just when the bus took a turn and the pressure from behind came with much stronger force. She looked behind a saw an elderly, bald man who winked and smiled at her. In a flash of second, she realized what the man was thinking. He was having a hard on and was fully taking advantage of the situation and was deriving dirty pleasure. She pulled her hockey stick and thumped on the ground with the intention of hitting the man. It worked, her stop came and she alighted from the bus. After this incident, she became more cautious and never boarded a loaded bus.. She narrated the incident to her mother. Her mother advised her to be bold enough keeping in mind the situation she is in. If she is in a crowd, she could think of giving back. On the other hand if she was alone, the best approach would be to ignore and try to reach for a safer place. She learnt that a girl who greets or smiles at co-passengers, society views it as an invitee.That day, some strange power seems to seep inside her which made her strong.

While riding a two wheeler for classes, she had to face the nasty comments of young boys on two wheelers. They would drive past her at crazy speed or would honk persistently. She learnt to ignore them like every other girl of her age did, Best was to slow down and let them pass or change her route if she found them to be following her.

College life was a roller coaster ride too. But she viewed problems as challenges and converted them into opportunities. She had to wear glasses in college due to myopia. Most of the boys used to make fun of her and made comments like, "Oh! You have four eyes, so you must be possessing extra clear vision now." Once, while on a college trekking trip, one of senior who was involved with her roommate tried to take advantage of her. She shared with her and convinced her to leave him and move ahead in life. Respecting and maintaining dignity of her fellow colleagues became a priority. No wonder she was chosen as the President of her college. This position brought her in contact with youth politicians. This moment changed her life forever. After winning the President's post, she was coaxed into throwing a party for her supporters. Little did she know, this was a game plan of her senior, the same who had misbehaved on the college trip. He was son of a famous politician who had never heard the two lettered word "No" in his life. His ego had been bruised and he was hell bent on destroying Joa.

At the party, there was music, drink and all type of cocktails were being served. The party was going well past midnight, when the trance was broken by screeching sound of police cars. In a matter of few minutes, the party scene metamorphosed into scene of crime. Somebody had given a tip to cops and they had come with a search warrant. On investigation, drugs were found and Joa got arrested. She was the host and was responsible for what was being served that evening. Her cries of pleading "Not guilty" fell on deaf ears. At this point, her father stepped in to support her. Hired the best lawyers and she was alleviated off the charges. One of her friend's gave testimony that the drugs were brought by the politician's son. Her father advised her not to press charges against the boy. That day she reaffirmed that she will be very careful in treading her path and will not blindly believe anyone. That night she had a long talk with her father about the ways and behavior of male species.

She was slight overweight and her physical appearance brought about many rejections at job place. Majority of firms wanted typical stereotyped females as shown in cover of magazines, those living in body conscious state. What was expected was a female candidate with slender frame, wearing smart dresses and footwear with appropriate makeup and hairdo. It was all about the exterior appearance. No one waited to see her credentials and achievements. Joa was not like one of them. She always wore comfortable clothes and footwear. She lived in a soul conscious state and was happy. Her parents had brought her up like a child and not as a boy or a girl. Only when she entered her teens, it dawned upon her that she was of the fairer sex. Well, there are many good work organizations which are on a look out for brainy females. She got a job in a reputed firm.

Life was going well for some time. Then, she lost her father in a car accident. Life is unpredictable. Some part of her left with her father. Being the only child, she wanted to perform the last right. Once, again family and society showed her the mirror that she was the weaker sex. The right to perform the last rights was the domain of a son. Her father will not be able to cross the next dimension which helps a soul in uniting with God. So her first cousin was chosen. She braved the situation well. With her mother's love and unconditional support, she voiced that when her father never brought about this topic, nobody else had the right to bring it up. Her parents were proud of her. Her mother supported her and stood firm by her decision. Joa did the last rights of her father. She realized her mother whom she thought was dominated by her husband (her father) had a voice of her own and was a strong willed lady. One's fragile frame is no way related to their inner strength. Mental strength is far more important, as life is a mental game.

Moving ahead in the latter half of third decade, a marriage proposal came from the man, the same boy who had testified in the drug case. She always believed she was not the typical marriage material. However, on her mother's counseling and perusal she tied the knot. Little did she know there were numerous chapters, far more challenging than ever before in the book of her life. Once, the suffix in law gets added to the woman of her new household, their behaviors changed. The boy's mother, who seemed to adore her when she had come with the marriage proposal for her son, now viewed her as a threat to her kingdom. Joa felt as if she was some witch luring her husband away from his mother. This is how exactly her mother in law behaved. The boy's sister who was showering with love earlier, now left no stone unturned to make sure that Joa realized their sibling relationship was way superior to Joa's married relationship. Whenever, her husband would bring her a gift, her sister in law would take it away by voicing it loud that it was for her as her brother loved his sister more than his wife. Her mother in law always stepped in to support this.

Her mother in law and sister in law would behave differently in Joa's husband presence and absence. These behavioral changes seemed to upset Joa a lot. On one hand, Joa was trying her best to strengthen her marriage bond with her husband and on the other hand she was being victim of gas-lighting. They played mental games with Joa which drained her and she ended up feeling sad and upset. It took her few years before she realized, this diplomacy was a way in her household. In front of Joa, her in-laws always complained about her husband and vice versa. This approach was brought to light by her husband when he had differences with his mother. He talked about his mother's behavior openly and how she tried to poison his mind against his own wife. This devastated Joa. Deep inside, she decided that she will stop reacting to these small petty fights.

Initial few years, Joa was busy with raising her children. There was no support from her in laws family. So she created her own support system of helpers. She pushed aside these incidents and involved herself in her profession and children. It seemed she had created an electrified invisible boundary. Who so ever tried to disturb her system, got an invisible shock. All through her married life journey, she shared in detail with her mother whenever she felt upset. Her mother always counseled her to focus on brighter side of life. The larger picture was, her husband loved her and they had two beautiful children.

Joa always felt like an outsider. It seemed to her as if she was not required and her job was to give an heir which had been accomplished. She kept herself busy in her professional work and later in taking care of children. Her sister in-law who had got married sometime in between, kept visiting the household too often and tried her best to control both the houses. Her focus was more on her family than her spouse's family. Usually, Joa was not aware of what was happening in her household. As her in-laws discussed everything with her sister in law even petty things like menu to be served if the guests came over. Her sister in law was always called for whenever guests came for serving and interaction. These things started piling up and Joa felt on the verge of nervous breakdown. Inspite, of spending a decade in this household, it was always about her husband and his sister. She could not see where she fitted in. She wondered whether this was how living with in-laws worked. There was so much of hypocrisy, diplomacy and melodramas. This thought sucked her and she started distancing herself from them.

Going for long walks or meditating were her ways to release the built up pressures. Normally, she would retire with a cup of tea on her terrace and introspect. Her favorite lines from her poster in her room flashed in her mind. "God give me courage to change the things, I can! Serenity to accept the things, I cannot change and Wisdom to know the difference between the two!"

This flashback moment propelled her forward with mightier force than ever. Finally, she could understand the depth of each word. She armed herself with three important tools – Courage, Serenity and Wisdom. From that moment she decided she will not let anyone or anything spoil her mental peace. Nothing was more important than her mental well being. She took a leap of faith and changed her orbit into a higher realm. From this higher orbit, she felt no emotions for people who had tortured her in various ways all through these years. She felt pity for them as they were spending this beautiful life form as human beings in doing petty things and picking up small fights. Their motto in life was to eat, drink, sleep and do loose talk about family members or friends. She could visualize that their life would be spent in doing this. People in slumber behaved like this. It was not her duty to awaken them up. Rather, it was the moment of awakening for her. With a heart full of gratitude, she forgave each one of them and felt a burden lift off her soul.

She felt new energy force from within. She resumed all that she used to love doing before her marriage. She sang songs, listened to music and started spending time with herself. The change was so obvious that nobody could escape sensing it. Her skin started to glow, there was a sprint in her walk and she seemed happy. Her children were overjoyed as they saw a happy, energetic mother as compared to tired, complaining mother. The romance in her married life was back and she felt very lucky and grateful. This change brought about a feeling of insecurity in her in laws family. They failed to understand her change, leave aside appreciate. They started weaving stories about Joa being in some extra marital relationship. What else had brought about this change? They tried to feed dirty thoughts in her husband's mind too but he discarded them. Joa realized, a strong minded, independent woman intimidates everyone and they see her as a threat. All their energy and efforts went in searching the source of her strength. Such small minded people can never realize that the strength always comes from inside. There is no source outside.

Joa realized majority of woman who live in joint families dealt with similar such issues which now seemed petty and insignificant to her. Although initially they had seemed so big, that she was almost about to crumble beneath its weight. In our society, one is never taught how to deal with day to day challenges. Nobody wants to share their own experiences and ways on how they overcame. Just as a new bride, faces adversities at the hand of her mother in law and sister in law, with the known fact that the mother in law was once a newly wedded bride too. She must have also faced difficult situations. But she chooses not to share and let the new bride go through the same mental trauma. How can we talk about women empowerment when the behavior of the same woman changes from mother to mother in law, sister to sister in law and daughter to daughter in law! Are these suffixes "in law" so powerful that they change the personality once tagged?

It's time to stop and think. The same woman who loves her daughter despises and shuns when a daughter is borne by her daughter in law. Why are such crimes still happening? The reason is obvious. Majority of women never really try to empower another woman. If one woman has failed to achieve something, there are slim chances that she will share her experiences with another woman for her benefit. So, she tries to discourage other woman on similar path or just behave the same way as people had behaved. This has to do with our judgemental society. No one wants to be judged. The root cause is this. If there is paradigm shift from being judgemental to unconditional acceptance, human relations will improvise. There are very good chances that this it will be bloom time on Mother Earth and there will be unconditional love, care and compassion.

Joa was now well versed with the usage of her three most powerful tools, courage, serenity and wisdom. She launched a Self help group site by the name, "Just Me". This was an interactive session group where woman could share their difficult times as anonymous and could unburden themselves or seek help. Request for discussions with Joa and counselors are encouraged so as no woman suffers even in the slightest way as Joa felt she did. In her place, a weak minded woman could have take any extreme step, be it of walking out of marriage to suicide.

In case of Joa, the woman who empowered her was, initially her mother and later her daughter. But what about thousands of woman out there with no digital access? To address this issue, volunteers from her group reach to various rural areas. They empower one woman and encourage her to create more groups and sub groups. Gradually, woman started opening up and started sharing their problems.

Joa's efforts are paying rich dividends as her group has started setting various sub groups in different cities of each state. Unconditional hearing and acceptance is the key to work as volunteer in these groups. There are strict privacy guidelines. Gradually, the message has started to spread like fire that till the time all women decide to unite, they will always be oppressed and suppressed by their counterpart species. Each woman should hold the baton to educate and empower one woman.

Time is not far when such words like women empowerment will disappear and both men and women will be respected for who they really are? They are the two most beautiful creations by God. The thought behind creating them is different, so how can be compare them? Each one is unique.

Joa is just another girl next door who was living an ordinary life and facing routine adversities. Thinking out of the box led to her transformation. She has helped numerous women so far. She runs a woman centric organization where the only qualification one needs is to be woman who is non-judgemental and is willing to listen and share.

Joa's favorite quotes are

"Helping others heal, is a path of self healing."

"One should never try to take control of life, Life is meant for sharing."

Poem By Ekta Singh Chandel

My Room Of Yours

Your watch on my bedside
Your hoodies peeping out from my cupboard
Creases on my bedsheet murmuring *i miss you*
View of your ass dancing effortlessly
Filling every corner of my room
Of my head
I wonder
How am I going to take it all
In this state, when I am most vulnerable
It's morning
And my room is breathing in your aroma
My table and chair, bathed in imprint
Of your hands
My doormat is waiting
As if you are the master
Your hat on the stand
Radiating more belongingness than my own
For once, I forget
Where I am
The longer

I watch you walking around

Naked and charming

In my room of yours

The truth resurfaces

It's me

My room of yours

Short Stories And Poem By Deep Wilson

Roots

Sitting in my balcony, every morning, sipping tea, looking across hill-tops, park below, early risers walking with flights hovering above, people on the move right from morning, with my pet sitting beside me, not knowing that Manju would never miss this sitting except when it would be chilly and windy. When windy sitting inside and through the window not lose the same morning.

Even though with a helping hand I managed the house-hold chores, recipes, cakes being one, I liked baking. Into such a fascination for cakes came to me from my grandparents, every Sunday, banana, pine-apple cakes, sweetened our togetherness, now with that still intact, I was moving on.

I would be ready, every morning, in formal wear as going to work before formal work hours, this I had picked up from my dad who would never be late in going to work.

My grandfather always meticulously dressed up I took on from him. My grandmother, always particular about her morning priorities, her ever nobility, I caught on.

I grew up seeing across, distinctly from my window, hill-tops, at a distance, summer-hill, with circular road, traffic at slow pace. Daily routine with meals dot on time, time was all priority, my grandparents never missed that.

My love for reading, as newspaper inevitably would be read, my grandfather reading, musing and looking across the window, every morning.

I grew up in a highly disciplined atmosphere, talk during our meals, very educative, my grandfather would reminisce and take me and my grandmother to his college and university days, off and on. My grandfather was very well-read, a thorough gentleman. After I would come back from college and later from university, he would sit with me after coming back from work and take me to my interests, my walk with books, would chip in and give his views. Never a day would go by when we would not sit and go into the world of knowledge. My admiration for him grew each day and what I admired about him was that he never interfered. He would never ask as to what I did during the day or what happened in the university. All that he did was to sit with me every evening with highly educative vistas.

He empowered me with right values right from my impressionable age. This was so much now ingrained in me that it had become my life.

On weekends my grandmother and my grandfather took me to our dear and near ones. We would sit with them and talk about the week gone by, never about others. Weekends would be outings too but more in the world of relationships. This strengthened each relationship.

I recall, how we all would sit with my parents and my three younger sisters would be part of the conversation.

I was a bit reserved but when I spoke, I spoke my mind, right from child-hood. As I grew up, words became paramount with me. I did think before I spoke. I made friends as all do but was quite selective.

I didn't like to be with those who jeered and mocked others, I liked those who made meaningful conversation, this was in me that I had picked up from my grandparents.

In college and university I was known as being frank and upright. I was friendly with all but close to those I liked more, our friendship lasted, still lasts. In our conversations we did go into the world of admiration as in life there are those who like and admire. We all moved on but with time we got immersed into our own world, our life's journey. Even when I moved on to open new vistas of my own family, I stayed in tune with my grandparents, with my parents, with my sisters. Wherever I would be, I kept on with them, I did lose contact with many I knew as work took precedence.

Momentum

In life we move on from familiar to unfamiliar lanes.

In our lane of professionalism we keep running the race, work hard, put in our best to achieve, to accomplish, with perseverance we climb all ladders, with our zeal to excel we reach the top, we are applauded, appreciated, recognition brings in confidence, we gain momentum to move on.

I had always been clear in my vision, that vision that took birth right through and through from the time I sat with educative mingling.

My priority, I didn't know then but I knew that one day I would be able to share my journey of my own priorities. No one knows what course life takes and we drift on. We keep on with our momentum and what shape that momentum would take we do not know. What we grow up with and what grips us we don't know.

I didn't know what was to come next and what time would come in when I would talk about not just my college days but added on all about what I learnt that I continued to move on with, all that I had imbibed through those who taught us I would make it known to the outside world.

Life is about relationships, from the time we are born, relationships bind us, our parents, our sister, our brother and we grow up with warm affection by each one, there is a chord of oneness that is stronger than the roots of a tree, these roots cannot be shaken by storms or whirlwinds. These pillars of warmth remain steadfast throughout and if at all during the course of life find patches of differences, ties still remain ever strong. We exist through this everlasting bond that boosts our morale, constantly.

With these roots that gave direction to my life, I was ready to take a plunge in the vast sea. I knew that I would be able to swim as through my roots I had learnt to swim across in calm or stormy sea.

I wanted to run with time and be on the go, on the move. Momentum, I wanted to stay on with my momentum. From school to college to university, now I was in the threshold of my professional life, I was on this cross-road, I had a vision but still I didn't know exactly what to take on, what to do and what not to do. This happens with each one of us throughout life. If we stay in tune with time and don't let it run faster than us then we can attain what we desire faster. We need to pause when it wants us to and when we pause we should make use of that to reenergize ourselves and move on with more enthusiasm.

Time had empowered me, what was ingrained in me through and through I would stay steadfast with. Time waits for no one, I had learnt and seen swiftness. Each minute, each second was precious and I would value that.

I would remain wide awake.

Accomplishments

I moved on with focus on what lay ahead, work priorities. I had always planned what to do during the day but now this needed exactness, more precision with absolute professionalism. Time had come in to let my ability surface. After getting ready for work, I took sometime to be with myself. I went into exact minutes of what I would do. I remembered when in college we organized a debate session and I never let even one minute go past all specifics.

This exactness to time was noticed early in my career and I was empowered with a position and with that came in a lot of responsibility. I knew that all work hard as all want to move up the ladder but time precision matters the most. Momentum can be regained but time when once lost cannot be regained. I took on this responsibility with more exactness. I now had a team with me and I needed to balance my work and lead the team as well.

A seminar, I conducted exclusively for women, my colleagues and empowered them with my thoughts:

Compatibility

We all work, work to achieve, work to accomplish, work to win, we keep building up our competence, we do get appreciation but we get so overwhelmed that we forget to run on the lane of compatibility, while running we see that there is no one behind, there is no one sitting in the stands, we then realize that we have not nourished the lane of compatibility, we change our lane forthwith and start running on the lane of compatibility, now we are delighted that the whole stadium is full and our well wishers are applauding, now we know which lane to run on, we feel so inspired on this lane, we can certainly run miles and miles on this lane of compatibility throughout and throughout.

Priorities

We begin the day with our daily routine, the formal work arena is our priority, we work with end in view, in the work arena there are competitive lanes, need constant run, after we come out from this competitive lane we are in total command of our priorities, these priorities are flexible and we can shift and change all order, even if our priority remains a priority we do not mind as no race, we are putting in our best and the wonderful part is that we are seeing our best alone, we are certain our priority will not remain a priority, we alone are running in this lane, no competition, we are certain we will always win as we own these priorities.

Exclusiveness

Over the years I have always emphasized on exclusiveness, a shopping mall fascinates everyone for its wonderful display and we buy things that are exclusive, the beautiful landscape and the eye catching snow-capped mountains win our hearts, a match we cheer and applaud not so much for the winning moves but for the different styles, exclusiveness is what matters.

Nature

Our close companion, Nature, the moment we are out in the open flowers greet us, we have no time to give the flowers company in the morning, we return the greetings in the evening with a smile, walk with greenery all around. Nature admires us for our loving nature for returning its warmth, desires freshness for us always, in darkness the twinkling stars brighten us, in winter Nature desires we absorb winter's sweetness not its bitter cold, feel the wonder of snowflakes, see the beauty of snow all around, in spring Nature promises all ecstasy, refreshes us. Nature promises happiness if and only if we never give up, conveys this wonderfully through its wonders, sunshine within we keep walking and smiling with Nature, certainly we never give up.

Stance

We need to have a proper stance to have a good outcome, we see players in all games and when we focus on their success we notice they concentrate on their stance before the game begins and even during the game, an athlete takes a stance, is ready at 'on your marks go' and moves instantly, be a sportsperson or professional or otherwise, stance is the most important, stance gives clarity of purpose.

Home

Everyday is a journey and everyday we undertake a journey where we spend most of our time, at our work place and the second journey with those we are closely associated with, the first journey takes us miles and miles, our second journey is a wonderful journey, a journey that too takes us miles and miles but with a difference, destination is 'home sweet home', so energizing, energy of oneness, energy of togetherness.

Mother

My Mother at Sixty-six by Kamala Das is a wonderful title, takes us to the ever warm world of the daughter and mother, the expression my Mother echoes deep emotions of oneness, of togetherness, of unfailing love, my Mother, my life, my world, as years roll by, sixty-six, feelings surface, dearer the person fear of parting grips us more and more and as we journey with these feelings we go into the depth of emotions, the daughter didn't want to see her mother in that state of paleness, wanted to see her cheerful, full of vigour and strength.

I took life in four stages, school, college and university, professional and fourth stage which I titled as Relationship stage.

In first, school stage, we win awards, certificates, trophies, mementoes. We proudly go up on stage to receive. We are applauded and that motivates us to move on with more accolades.

Next stage, college and university, we learn more and more about life's wins.

All of us have a benchmark and this benchmark we need to stay on with throughout. Evaluation of our benchmark is done externally here but the benchmark we desire in life is done internally by us alone. We alone can determine our strengths and weaknesses and turn our weaknesses into strengths. We can unlock our strengths with our key and nurture them.

In our third stage, professional arena, we delve into the formal world. Work is our be all and end all during that time. We are recognized for our work and with those incentives we keep on with more and more to come.

In our fourth stage, Relationship stage, we get into compatibility and try to regain our lost connections due to our work focus. We can walk at our own pace, our evening side-walk is so refreshing, those jogging move ahead, we don't mind as no competition intended. Those driving stop when they see us crossing and give way, we too need to give way and then again maintain that pace.

During all these stages one thing is common with all of us, we have been appreciated and with that appreciation we gather momentum. One thing with few of us in the fourth stage is complacency and that catches on with us.

What we have gained in earlier three stages we need to keep those alive in the fourth stage and not let our achievements go into oblivion. This is the stage when all that we have been empowered with we can pass on, share our expertise, our expertise had empowered us and we can now empower others with this expertise which is real life-time experience.

Our titles that we have won we can substantiate with meaningful entities and give direction to a meaningful life to all those in the threshold of a career and let meaningful content flow on. Contents that come in through experience are profound and realistic.

We were empowered through our roots and we can further empower others through our expertise and meaningful experiences.

Life's journey only the one who goes through that journey knows exactly what it portrays. We have gone through that journey, let others benefit from that. Then all accomplishments will stay wide awake.

Life's Windows

From my balcony, those hill-tops reminded me of those tunnels in those hills, more than hundred in number. It had been years and I wanted to feel the experience, to see how these tunnels remained in momentum ever.

It didn't take long for me to hop in that majestic train and as I hopped in a voice called out, my name, Manju.

I looked behind, seated in there, smiling was my child-hood friend, Neelam. We had lost contact as both of us were engrossed in our world of work and family. Both of us could see the joy in not just seeing each other but now that we could journey together and reminisce.

As the first tunnel approached we went into our days gone by. We delved into each moment right from the time we were together in school, our schooldays brought in smiles and laughter. Each one of our family as we were family friends too. She opened by asking about those steps leading to my place where I grew, where we would go up and down those steps and then run outside, take the steps, reach Baljees of then and from there turn, keep running and go up the Ridge and play on those benches.

Those days when my grandmother would call her over and on Sunday we would have fun and not miss cake puddings, prepared by her.

We grew up together, same college, same university, same friends with a few different, so much to talk about, so much to share, will those more than hundred tunnels be enough for more than a thousand realities of life. Maybe not but we were ecstatic that we had met, we had lost touch but we knew about each other's life's journey. We knew that webs did emerge during the course of our journey as all face but without saying we knew we would not brood over that. Without saying we knew we had left all that behind. Without saying we knew we would delve into our accomplishments and make our journey as splendid as the scenic splendour that all these tunnels saw each morning, not looking at the darkness in the tunnel but at the horizon each morning, looking at the twinkling stars every evening, keeping their home bright.

As tunnels came in one after another we didn't miss a moment, even that which it seemed we had forgotten, came back to life.

Our going to college together, then in the gaps in between for next class go on that lonely stretch in the company of trees and gentle breeze. With more friends coming in we would sit on the pavement and on the curve see cars moving in and out through the college entrance. Life had taken a full circle, we didn't know then that those days would surface and we would cherish those moments.

Fifty number flashed as we looked outside. We could not escape the beautiful expanse outside, stone walled cottages on hills, could see in lonely stretches women carrying loads on their back, stretching themselves to earn a living. It didn't matter to them when it rained or hailed but they kept on and hailed in their hale of winning at the end of the day. With renewed vigour and strength they took on the next mantle of momentum each day, seen by others or not seen, it did not matter to them. To them all that mattered was making two ends meet. Appreciation came in or not, it did not demoralise them. What did they understand about name flash, what did they understand about promotions. They didn't know with success attitudes of others change, they didn't know about perspectives, they didn't know about priorities. All they knew was about house-hold chores, their life revolved around that. They didn't get bewildered by those who desired to make this as a priority for them. They were proud of the work they were doing. The train whistled on sharp turns, we looked outside.

Each day life quickens its pace. We have our priorities and we run along with these priorities, each one has different perspective and priorities of each vary. Could be for one recognition and appreciation, for another to accomplish, yet for another to fulfill their needs. We focus on one aspect and we drift on with that, we choose a path or mid-path and try to remain in control of that. These hill-women have chosen a path to keep themselves going and that is what gives them direction. If they keep going on, their wants too will be fulfilled and for this reason we often see them merrily swaying, singing along, binding the grain.

We are reminded of the Solitary Reaper by William Wordsworth.

"Behold her, single in the field,

Yon solitary Highland Lass!

Reaping and singing by herself;

Stop here, or gently pass!

Whate'er the theme, the Maiden sang

As if her song could have no ending;

I saw her singing at her work,

And o'er the sickle bending;-

I listened, motionless and still;

And, as I mounted up the hill,

The music in my heart I bore,

Long after it was heard no more."

A tunnel turn took us to those days, the train to Summer-hill, the University slope, smiles and greetings, we were getting to know that greetings mattered in life, greetings inspire, greetings bring in compatibility, greetings keep all associations alive, we didn't know then that if we empower ourselves with greetings we can meet one day.

Today, I wanted to relive my walk, my sprint, my marathon and my crossing the finishing line with applause.

As we approached a cross road, loud whistle, even those half-asleep, through their window looked outside, all were now wide awake, seemed a few were awe-struck by the scenic wonder and many seemed lost in their own train of thoughts. In life no one knows what goes on in one's mind.

With each turn, we went into all turns, all sharp turns. She murmured about certain webs and how she came out from those webs. We looked outside. With gentle breeze blowing we flew into years of praise and admiration. We wanted to overshadow all our impressions and not only impressions but situations that did jolt us. I plunged into the vast sea, that sea where I learnt to swim, that ship that took me to calm waters and did not let me get drowned in the world of obsessions. Rather the world that had empowered me. I had never been extravagant and lavish but today I was into all extravagance and lavish in my praise of those who showed me newness in life.

I wondered if my friend was listening to me or was relating all this with her own world. Our life's experiences were similar and it did not matter if we were listening to each other. All mattered was that our windows were open and the gentle breeze was taking in our life's marathons. We were not looking for responses or nods. We desired to echo our accomplishments, our pinnacles of success. Webs we wanted to leave behind as we had done to move on, we had subdued all that could be demoralising with our achievements, we had opened new chapters in our life, those webs now submerged, blessing in disguise as those webs motivated us, gave us that vital push and vigour to move ahead with all momentum. Webs do give a push but webs too teach us to stay away from these and not get entangled for when we get entangled we lose right perspective. We need to feel inspired not through episodes but through meaningful roots.

Tunnels were closing in but life's windows were still opening up.

The canopy of shrubs and herbs we could see throughout. In the backdrop of this canopy stand tall age-old trees. Most of them are hundreds of years old. They have stood the test of time and continue to mesmerize us with their grace. The landscape is made ethereal with these trees Pine and Deodar, the cones present on these trees give magnificence to this world. The sun brings in warmth and brightness. In our lives too each day a Mother brings in warmth and brightness, she is so sublime, full of life. She gives all her world to her children, her priorities are none. She desires only the well-being of her children, sacrifices everything, she is epitome of self-sacrifice. What can her children give her in return for all that she does, even if they try, they will not be able to as it goes beyond all comprehension. She desires health for her children, a treasure beyond all treasures.

All in there were nodding, it seemed they were listening, all were wide awake.

Relationship

The last tunnel opened into mountains of togetherness. On reaching, we walked up the slope together and on reaching the circular road we continued with our journey on life's circular road. On crossing the victory tunnel I thought what I had won to feel victorious, if at all. I walked up the slope, I paused, stood right infront of the Hall of Fame from where I had started my life's journey. I had come back full circle. I could through my life's window, reflect.

Have we won and do we feel empowered with our wins?

We can feel empowered when we know exactly what a win is. Win is not in attaining positions, win is not in getting accolades. Win is when, as mother, as sister, as spouse, we accept, which as mother we do and that is, win. Then only we can feel empowered, only then we can empower others.

Empowering and wins is not in one aspect but numerous, such as, those hill-women carrying loads on their back, they had empowered themselves with wins of hard work each day.

Those were the days when work priorities took us to distant lands, with my life's bonding, my family, my spouse, my children. I had worked hard as all do. I didn't want to lose that. I had climbed all ladders. I was never distant with my vision, my goals to achieve. At every step, every position that I attained, I felt it was not positions that flashed but what I had learnt and passed on, meaningful titles that I had empowered others with.

I had never become complacent and I didn't want to be complacent now as well. Complacency would nil all that I had put in through all my efforts and hard work, I wanted to remain wide awake and not let any experience of mine go waste. Each minute I wanted to make use of by keeping alive all that had given me the confidence to move on. I didn't want to put my letters of appreciation, my trophies, my mementoes in closets, our certificates neatly tacked or enclosed in albums. I wanted to keep all alive, through the same way, same routine, same timings, same work ethics. My name flash at that time on my office was not just for that moment to be proud of and let that fade away. That name flash didn't come in easily, it came in with a lot of toil, that toil that came in with a mix of so many aspects. One does feel empowered when in office but positions do not last, what lasts till we want is our momentum and I had empowered myself with that vital momentum. Getting empowered is not just in one aspect, that is, positions but all that has an impact and further motivates others to empower themselves with meaningfully. In our work lane we all try to empower ourselves through various wins but empowering ourselves not with wins but with reasons behind those wins is empowering. I wanted to stay on with those reasons that brought in those wins. My roots were intact which I continued to nourish. I wanted these roots to bloom and when I would see them blooming at this stage in my life when I was off from all name flash then that would be my life's accomplishment. I wanted to echo our milestones. Milestones stay with us. Even when we are off from our formal lanes, milestones, each moment inspire.

We immersed in our world of honour and respect, of our name flash that mattered at that point in time as that brought in a sea change in attitudes.

I wanted to look back that gave us the impetus to move on. Those times when for an event I desired all my women colleagues come in with all magnificence, in all similarity of momentum. All applauded, all cheered, the arena resonated, resonated seeing our momentum. Momentum matters in life, accomplishments flash but momentum flashes throughout.

When every summer I would come in from distant lands I could see distance had become distant, doors of warmth opened, through cordiality windows I could feel the breeze of togetherness. I wondered if name flash mattered, I wondered if pedestal of success mattered. My friend, nodded.

I wanted to go back to those steps, steps of my journey right from the beginning. Now, I was right there and I wanted to feel life again. I wanted to go into that ecstasy of tapping those doors again, those doors that were with me throughout my journey and share with them not about the pages they knew but about the pages that came in with all newness to me.

Worn out pages I wanted to leave behind, obstacles trounce, webs denounce, only wins and wins announce, only accomplishments echo far and wide, these accomplishments subdue all tides, see rainbow through all tunnels, silver linings on each cloud, snow-capped mountains, hill-tops laden with greenery, gentle breeze, ever flowing, empowering all with ever freshness, keeping all wide awake.

Gracious

Wide awake she as Mother
Wide awake she as Sister
Everyday wealthier
Seeing her children merrier
Everyday empowering her children
With inspiration
Each day her children empowering her
With appreciation
To her children, is precious
To her spouse, is gracious
With her sisters always gentle
Takes on each mantle
With all perfection
Nobility her mansion
Each day wide awake
Ever on move
Nothing to prove
Nothing asks in return
Nothing as much can be given
In turn

We empower her with our salute

Our salute

Ever wide awake

Wide awake

My Son's Letter To Me

Happy Mother's Day!

Thank you for being the watchful and classy protector, the pillar of strength and hope for all of us. I owe a lot of my professional success to the support and guidance you have provided me over the years. Your work ethics and dedication is one of the best I have seen growing up.

Thank you for being you.

This letter from my son, keeps me WIDE AWAKE

Empowered Strong Women

Not long ago, in distant land, my daughter, in desperation, my daughter in fear of losing her very own, her very own sweet smiling daughter, the young one braving it out with all smiles, the family torn between home and medical advice. I flew in, what could I give to my daughter, I was helpless, seeing my daughter in agony. I had come in a long way with my roots and now this was the time to do something for my root but I was helpless. One evening, on a call, we were to immediately reach in as time was failing us, frantically we moved out, looking for a cab, my son-in-law had already driven in and was doing what he could do but he too was helpless. Time was running out and with my daughter I was running desperately for a cab. As it would have it, a cab stopped and agreed to take us on, swiftly. Time failed us but time too gave us strength and what was ingrained in me through my roots to face all odds in adversity, I passed on, strengthened my daughter, words cannot console at such a time but roots that never show, can.

My roots, I furthered on, strengthened my family to stay with roots ever strong, even in adversity stay WIDE AWAKE.

About the Authors

Tanmayi Arora

Tanmayi Arora, is a professional content writer, and a blogger. She believes writing is a powerful sword through which you can wage a war of words. It is an expression and catharsis of emotions for her. Writing uplifts her mood and is a great venting-out mechanism for her. What if you have nobody to talk to, simply create a story and tell your inner self of what & how it feels. There is no other way better than writing, in order to know oneself and speak to oneself.

Rojalin Mahapatro

Rojalin Mahapatro is a budding writer who writes in order to calm down the thoughts which are swirling in her mind like hurricane. Her poems have been published in some anthologies. She is pursuing Bsc in Computer Science. You can reach out to her via Twitter on *@rmahapatro8* or you can read her writings on Instagram - *@wavvyyy_xd*

Shruti Sinha

Shruti completed her graduation 10 years ago, is fond of reading, writing and painting. She likes to go out with her friends and loves listening to music.

Vidya Premkumar

Vidya was the former head of the department and assistant professor of English at Mithibai college for 17 years, with a cumulative teaching experience of 22 years. With a new leash to life after battling cancer last year, she decided to dedicate her time to writing and painting, her other two life long passions. She has published her works in various anthologies and online journals and has also contributed research articles to books, journals and conferences. She now lives in Wayanad with her partner and two cats.

Sristi Sengupta

Sristi is eccentric. Far too many people to vouch-safe for it but truly in the liveliest way possible. She is a traveler (solo), poet (novice), novelist (recently turned) and a dreamer! She has a knack for start ups and loves working with different ideas, especially in data and marketing. Her stories encompass her love for the ordinary and the way all that's around us, is also all what's inside. She is a woman and has no idea what would become of her if she wasn't one, raised by her kind.

Priyanka Joshi - More

Priyanka Joshi - More has authored academic papers which she has either published in books or the proceedings of the various national and international conferences she presented in. She had completed her high school at Georgetown American School, Guyana, South America. She has travelled to 12 countries. She completed her college and post-graduation and PhD in History from Pune. Currently, she is a college teacher and subject counsellor at the Savitribai Phule Pune University. Recently she has won accolades for Best Top100 Researchers in India and Best Teacher Awards 2022. Apart from her academic interests, she likes to write fiction - prose and poetry. She wishes to publish her novels in the future. She has multiple hobbies to unwind after a tiring day.

Dipayan Chakrabarti

Dipayan Chakrabarti is a creative writer hailing from India. His works have received numerous awards and have been published in several literary journals over North America, Europe, and Asia.

Juju's Pearls

Juju's Pearls (Dr. Reemanshu Goel Bansal) is a blogger, writer, social worker, traveler, counselor and a Radiologist. She describes herself as a wandering soul with a mission to make a difference during her mortal journey. Her first book "Momsie Popsie Diary - Tea time chitchat on living life" is Winner of Literary award 2022. Book ranked #2 on Amazon Hot new bestseller. Nominated for "Reader's Choice awards 2022," TCK Publishing, USA and NDWBF 2022 (New Delhi world book fair). She has co-authored four anthologies.

Savour fresh brews from her "My mind's cafe" at reemanshu.blogspot.com

Email: reemanshu2003@gmail.com

Instagram: reemanshubansal

Ekta Singh Chandel

Ekta Singh Chandel is a part time blogger, a part time storyteller, a part time poet and a part time thinker. Through the ups and downs of adulthood, she has been working on her debut fiction novel. She aims to pen down her every thought.

Connect with her at, Instagram - *@iektaaaa*

Deep Wilson

Mr. Deep Wilson is the author of Beyond Lines, he is a prolific writer and a highly acclaimed Educationist with decades of experience in senior roles. The author can be contacted at *beyondlineswriters@gmail.com*.

www.ingramcontent.com/pod-product-compliance
Lightning Source LLC
LaVergne TN
LVHW041851070526
838199LV00045BB/1544